# Camping

*In memory of my precious dad*
*John Ferguson*

*- his footprint gone from earth*
*handprint forever on my heart -*

*With special thanks to Marsha, Glenn Stuart and Gary-*
*who've shared with us their equipment, their knowledge, and their love of camping-*
—Nancy


*Merci Sasha, Mariah, and Lee —*

*For Nancy's father.*

—Brian

Text copyright © 2002 by Nancy Hundal
Illustrations copyright © 2002 by Brian Deines

Design by Wycliffe Smith

Published in Canada by Fitzhenry & Whiteside, 195 Allstate Parkway, Markham, Ontario L3R 4T8

Published in the United States by Fitzhenry & Whiteside, 121 Harvard Avenue, Suite 2, Allston, Massachusetts 02134

10 9 8 7 6 5 4 3 2 1

U.S. Publisher Cataloging-in-Publication Data
(Library of Congress Standards)

Hundal, Nancy.
Camping / by Nancy Hundal ; illustrated by Brian Deines. — 1st ed.
[32] p. : col. ill. ;   cm.

Summary: From the moment their campsite is established, the family slowly begins
to discover the magic of life in the wild. Nights so quiet and dark, it's like being wrapped in a blanket.
Food that warms the stomach and awakens the senses; swimming in the lake,
climbing trees and lolling in the sun. And millions, no, bajillions of stars.
ISBN 1-55041-668-5
ISBN 1-55041-728-2 (pbk)
1. Camping— Fiction.  2. Family life — Fiction.  I. Deines, Brian, ill.  II. Title.
[E]  21  2002  AC  CIP


National Library of Canada Cataloguing in Publication Data

Hundal, Nancy, 1957-
Camping

ISBN 1-55041-668-5 (bound).—ISBN 1-55041-728-2 (pbk.)

I. Deines, Brian  II. Title.

PS8565.U5635C34 2002        jC813'.54        C2002-900338-5
PZ7.H899Ca 2002

# Camping

BY NANCY HUNDAL
ILLUSTRATED BY BRIAN DEINES

FITZHENRY & WHITESIDE

Holidays, lolling days.
Mom wishes for museums and art galleries.
Dad talks about fancy hotels. My sister Laurie
wants malls. Duncan dreams of arcades.

And I long for Disneyland.

But money is scarce, so we'll try camping.
No paintings or fluffy towels, no clothes racks,
jackpots or mouse ears.

Camping.
Mosquito bites,
burnt food.
Camping.

Car packed, car stacked.

Freeway Entrance - speed up.

Exit Right to Highway - slower.

Merge Left - graveled laneway - crawling.

Tent up.
Cloth spread, poles tensed, home raised.
My sleeping bag, pillow, teddy. A playhouse for day,
a flimsy fortress at night. Yawning space beyond.

No houses, no street lamps, nobody. Tree to tree, we
string ropes for beach towels, dishtowels, and for garbagey
treats slung out of raccoon reach.

Chairs out,
kindling in,
tent flap down,
feet up.

Campfire, first night.
Bits of wood, a few pinecones, a couple of sticks.

My stomach shivers, thinking of camp food. Blech.
But mmm...chicken stew and hot, creamy marshmallows.
The black charry bits scabbed to stick, stuck to fingers.
Burnt.

Mmm. Camp food.

That night, I peep from the tent. Black, so black.
Even with eyes adjusted, the black tucks so carefully
around woodpile, between stumps, under trees.
Only memory rumples the blanket of darkness,
finds their places for me.

Hello? Anybody home?
For I am in their home now, camped
out in a deer's living room,
swimming in a raccoon's kitchen.
Pull head back, burrow into sleeping bag.
Listen to the black, gaze at the silence.
Sleep.

In the morning, I try a sip of coffee, boiled over the fire.
Roll its hard, hot taste over my tongue. But Mom and Dad
say Mmmmm, and grip their mugs like treasures.

Smoke from the fire teases me, tracks me. In a chair,
on the ground, by the tent. Nose poked, eyes pierced.
We play tag and it wins.

We work.
Chop wood, gathered from a pile at camp's center.
The woodpile spills with a thousand different shapes - a face,
a frog, a flute. Hard to gather when there's so much to see.

Then water from the pump. I push with my whole body,
hang over the handle. But still it only jerks halfway down.

When Dad pushes, the creaking metal finally says *yes*,
brings up its chilling water. Such hard won water tastes good.

And dishes. Hot water suds
in a bucket, sometimes done
late, late at night - by touch,
not sight.

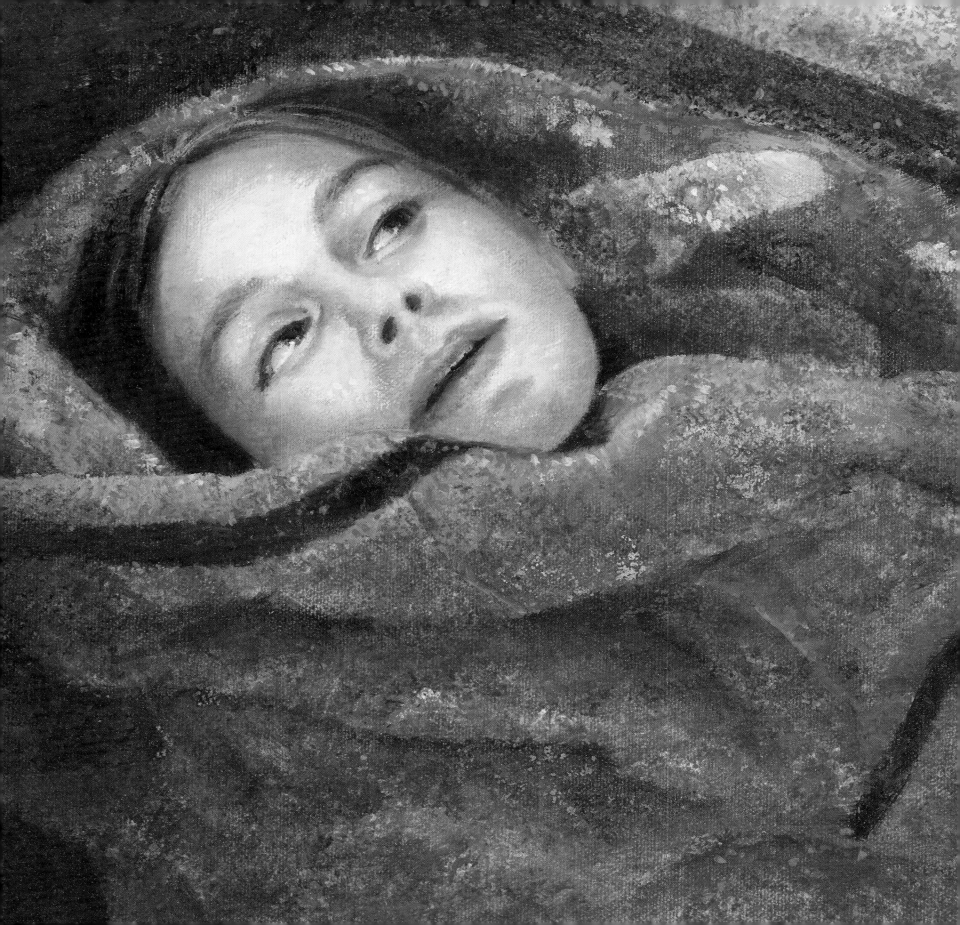

The quiet, so quiet.
Except for cars crawling by, gravel-crunching,
looking for the best spot. The slow building *tooooot*
of a train, which blows only at night. Or do we only hear it
at night? And the *swoosh* of cars on the highway, too busy
to stop. These sounds are distant, unimportant. Even the call
of the mall to Laurie is faint, Duncan's arcade symphony
ceases to jangle, and I forget all about the mouse ears,
listening for me.

Just a voice call, door slam, chipmunk chatter, wood axed.

And the quiet, so quiet.

We swim in the lake, dock bobbing with the sway of water.
We are used to the pool, not this green cool, fish school.
Plant tendrils catch in our hair; fine mud webs our toes.
We gasp for air,  horrified, delighted.

Hot days, warm evenings, chilled nights, cool mornings.
The breeze, fluttering the leaves in a thousand tiny *hi's*,
lifts my hair. The snow still sticks to mountain peaks and
waits for winter, with green violet trees spread below.

We feel the sun's journey across our campsite.
It taps our tent in the morning, pours like syrup warm
and thick at noon. By evening, gentle fingertips
of light massage the trees goodnight.

Doing nothing. Mom reads. Dad snoozes.
Laurie stares at the sky. Duncan watches ants on parade.
I stare down a mosquito.

Doing nothing. It's good.

Evenings around the fire, wrapped to my ears in a blanket.
Bug guard, chill guard, both try to sneak past to my skin.
Hot chocolate warms lips, throat, stomach, hands.

We sing old songs, new songs, camp songs, Gramp songs.

More chips, more sun, less TV, less washing.

More time, less o'clock.

I find a friend at a nearby site.
We run up and down camp lanes,
no traffic to fear.

Watch an eagle sail slowly on currents
of air that touch our freckled cheeks below.

Climb trees, play cards, stand still as a deer when that deer
sees us.

Hike through an old forest. Drive for ice cream to a new town.
Stores! Money! Let's go back to camp.

And at night, the tall trees ringing the campsite
point the way to the stars.
The stars!
Millions,
bajillions,
quadrillions, stream from one end
of the sky to the other.

Street lamps for the earth.

And then, the holidays are over.

No museum, no hotel, no mall, no arcade, no Disneyland.

But now we are campers. And we'll be back to stroll
and sing and scavenge.

Do nothing. And soon.